CREATURES FROM UFO'S

CREATURES FROM UFO'S

Daniel Cohen

Illustrated with photographs and drawings

DODD, MEAD & COMPANY
NEW YORK

The following illustrations are used by permission and through the courtesy of: Columbia Pictures, 17, 18; George W. Earley, 69; Mount Wilson and Palomar Observatories, 14; United Press International, 29, 33, 46, 55, 77. The drawings on pages 11, 25, 44, 53, 75, 83, 99, and 102 are by Donn Albright.

Copyright © 1978 by Daniel Cohen
All rights reserved
No part of this book may be reproduced in any form without permission in writing from the publisher
Printed in the United States of America

3   4   5   6   7   8   9   10

Library of Congress Cataloging in Publication Data

Cohen, Daniel.
  Creatures from UFO's.

  Includes index.
  SUMMARY: Discusses sightings of UFO's and encounters with creatures purportedly from those space crafts.

  1. Flying saucers—Juvenile literature. [1. Unidentified flying objects] I. Title.
TL789.C6518   001.9'42   78-7730
ISBN 0-396-07582-7

**In memory of Ray Palmer,
who first got me interested
in flying saucers**

CONTENTS

1 VISITORS FROM SPACE? 9
2 THE SOCORRO, NEW MEXICO, LANDING 20
3 THE FLYING SAUCER CRASH 30
4 THE NEW HAMPSHIRE KIDNAPPING 39
5 THE MISSISSIPPI FISHERMEN 51
6 THE ARIZONA WOODCUTTER 61
7 MOTHMAN 70
8 THE MYSTERIOUS MEN IN BLACK 81
9 CLOSE ENCOUNTERS IN OTHER LANDS 96
INDEX 110

1

VISITORS FROM SPACE?

On the evening of September 12, 1952, two teenagers in the small town of Flatwoods, West Virginia, saw a bright light in the sky. It looked like a meteor flash. The light disappeared behind a nearby hill.

The boys decided to take a look. They got a few of their friends and one adult and climbed the hill. At the top they said they found "a fire-breathing monster, ten feet tall with a bright green body and blood-red face." The creature floated toward them. The little group panicked. They ran madly down the hill and called the sheriff.

The sheriff went up the hill to investigate but he found nothing. The sheriff didn't believe the story and said so.

That is the tale of the Flatwoods Monster. It is one of the best-known accounts of what is supposed to be a meeting between people and creatures from a UFO.

A lot of people said that the flash of light in the sky had been made by a spaceship. The creature, they said, had come out of the spaceship. But a lot of other people agreed with the sheriff. They thought that the whole thing was made up.

Perhaps the story *was* made up, but not made up deliberately. Perhaps the group that went up the hill got overexcited. Maybe they only imagined they saw a monster. We have no way of knowing exactly what happened.

But the tale of the Flatwoods Monster is only one of hundreds of stories like it. Some of them are even stranger.

Take what was supposed to have happened at 2:30 A.M. on October 27, 1975, near Poland Springs, Maine. Two young men were driving along when suddenly they discovered they could no longer control their car. The car took

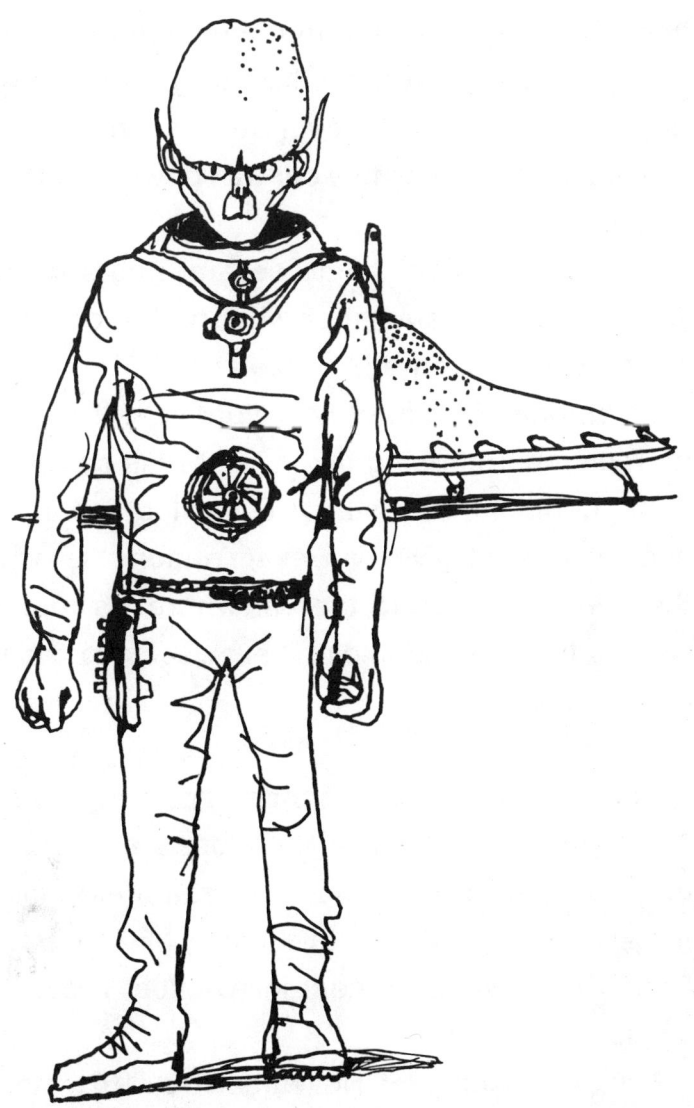

Many people have reported seeing strange creatures stepping out of UFOs.

them along a back road that they did not know and up to a lake. Near the lake they saw a large object shaped like a cylinder rise from the ground. Then their whole car was covered with a strange fog.

The two men got home several hours later. They could not remember what had happened after the fog appeared.

Later, one of the men was hypnotized. He said he remembered being taken out of his car by a strange-looking little man. He was led aboard a spacecraft and given an examination. He was then brought back to the car where his friend was waiting. His friend didn't even seem to know he had been gone.

Sometimes there are reports of meetings with strange creatures, but no UFOs are seen. Today most people assume that the creatures came from UFOs anyhow. The tale told by Mr. and Mrs. Peter Eilbes, who live near Milwaukee, Wisconsin, is an example.

On the evening of November 10, 1975, the doorbell of their house rang. Mrs. Eilbes answered it. She saw a very strange creature standing on her doorstep. The thing looked like a man wearing a small hat. But it was a very odd-looking man. The face was the color of "smoked meat." There were many gray lines on the face. The mouth was tiny, less than an inch wide. In its claw-like hand the creature held a long white rod.

The woman called her husband. He thought someone was playing a trick on them. He grabbed at the creature. It hit the ground with the rod. Then it floated back out of reach.

Mr. and Mrs. Eilbes slammed the door and looked out the window. They saw four more of the things. They were jumping around the lawn and street. Before they jumped they would hit the ground with the rod. The creature that had been on the doorstep waved its claw at them.

These are the types of stories you are going to read about in this book. They are stories about creatures that are supposed to have come out of UFOs.

People have been seeing strange creatures for thousands of years. People have also been seeing strange things in the sky for a very long

Is there intelligent life in outer space? Most scientists believe that there is.

time. But in 1947 a man named Kenneth Arnold was flying his plane in the state of Washington. He said he saw a number of round craft near the mountains. He had never seen anything like them before. Arnold said they moved "like a saucer skipping across the water." People started calling them "flying saucers." Sometimes they are still called flying saucers. More and more people began saying that they saw strange craft in the sky. Some of these craft did not look saucer-like. So a new name was invented. The name was Unidentified Flying Objects, or UFOs. UFOs can be pronounced "U-foes." People who are interested in UFOs call themselves "Ufologists."

The term Unidentified Flying Objects can be a little confusing. Everyone would agree that people see things in the sky that they cannot identify. But most people who say they "believe in UFOs" really believe that they have identified the objects. They think that UFOs are spaceships from other planets.

If UFOs are spaceships, then isn't it possible that there is somebody, or something, inside the ships? Isn't it also possible that sometimes the spaceship occupants are seen?

Millions of people all over the world have reported seeing UFOs. Not nearly as many have reported seeing creatures from UFOs. But such reports are still fairly common. Reports where UFO occupants are seen are called Close Encounters of the Third Kind. Close Encounters of the First Kind are reports where people see only a UFO. Close Encounters of the Second Kind are reports of physical evidence of a UFO sighting or landing. Close Encounters of the Third Kind are the rarest, but they are the ones that attract the most attention. The term "Close Encounters of the Third Kind" was also used as the title for a very popular movie about UFOs.

In this book we are going to look at some of the very best reports of Close Encounters of the Third Kind. By best, I mean the reports that have been investigated carefully.

Can we believe these reports? Are spaceships from other worlds really visiting our planet regularly? Are strange creatures getting out of these spaceships and walking or floating around the Earth?

Before we can answer yes to such questions we must be very careful. We have to look at the

Scenes from the popular science-fiction movie, *Close Encounters of the Third Kind.* The film shows what it might be like to meet creatures from space.

Other scenes from the movie, *Close Encounters of the Third Kind.* Seeing creatures from UFOs is the rarest kind of encounter.

evidence. Don't forget, at one time a lot of people said they saw ghosts. A lot of people also once said they saw unicorns and dragons. Creatures from outer space sound more up-to-date than dragons. But they are not necessarily any more real.

We must judge a report by the evidence. We must not believe something just because it is exciting. In the stories to follow you will be given the evidence. You be the judge of it.

But whether you "believe" or not, the stories are often exciting, and always strange. I think that you will enjoy them.

2

THE SOCORRO, NEW MEXICO, LANDING

Lonnie Zamora was a police officer in the town of Socorro, New Mexico. At a quarter to six in the evening of April 24, 1964, Zamora spotted a car speeding in the town. He began to chase the speeder.

About a mile outside of town Zamora heard a roar and saw a flash of light. He knew that dynamite was stored in a shed nearby. Zamora was afraid there had been an explosion. He stopped chasing the speeder to investigate the noise and the light.

The policeman turned off onto a little-used side road. He was looking for the dynamite

Lonnie Zamora

shack, but he saw something else. Several hundred feet away was a "shiny type object." At first it looked like an overturned car. He thought there had been an accident. He stopped his car to get a better look.

What Zamora saw then was to make UFO history. He said he saw "two people in white coveralls very close to the object. One of these persons seemed to turn and look straight at my car and seemed startled—seemed to jump somewhat." The two people did not look like they were wearing space suits or unusual uniforms. Zamora added, "These persons appeared normal in shape—but possibly they were small adults or large kids."

Zamora got on his car radio. He contacted State Patrolman Sam Chavez and said he was investigating a possible auto accident. Chavez set off to help Zamora, but Chavez took a wrong turn and was a little late in arriving.

Zamora continued driving toward the object. Part of the time he could not see it. His view was blocked by small hills. When he was about 100 feet away he stopped his car. He got out to take a good look.

Up close the thing no longer looked like an overturned car. It was white and egg-shaped. It seemed to be standing on girder-like legs. He could see no windows or doors and the two figures had disappeared.

Zamora took about three steps toward the strange object. Then he heard a very loud roar. Flame appeared under the object. The thing began to rise straight up into the air.

Lonnie Zamora had never seen anything like

this before. He thought there was going to be an explosion. He ran back in the direction of his car. He actually bumped into the car and knocked off his glasses. Zamora didn't stop running until he was about 200 feet away from the thing. Only then did he look back. But without his glasses he could not see very well.

When the object got about ten feet above the ground the flame vanished. The roar changed to a low whine. Then the object became silent. It moved off toward the southwest, hovering about ten feet above the ground. Finally it disappeared into the distance.

With the thing gone Zamora recovered a bit. He returned to his car and found his glasses. He then got back on the radio and called headquarters. He told the radio operator to "look out the window, to see if you can see an object."

A few seconds later Sergeant Chavez arrived. He found Zamora still very upset by his experience. The two men went down to where the strange object had stood. They found four marks in the ground. Zamora thought the marks had been made by the craft's legs. Some of the brush near the landing site had been burned. Zamora said it must have burned when the craft took off.

Some other marks were found in the area. Some people said they might be the footprints of the two men in white. Others suggested the marks might have been made by a ladder. The occupants might have needed a ladder to get in and out of their craft.

The Socorro, New Mexico, UFO landing became very famous. Within a few days people from all over the country came to Socorro. They talked to policeman Lonnie Zamora. They went out to look at the place where the spaceship was supposed to have landed. Many of them wrote stories and articles about what had happened.

Most Ufologists consider this case one of the best on record. But the case has one big flaw. The only person who saw the craft and its two occupants was Lonnie Zamora. Everyone in the area was asked if they had seen a strange craft on April 24, 1964. No one said they had.

There was one secondhand report from a man who worked in a gas station nearby. He said that a stranger had come into his station on April 24. This stranger said he had seen a silvery craft hovering above the ground. The time was just

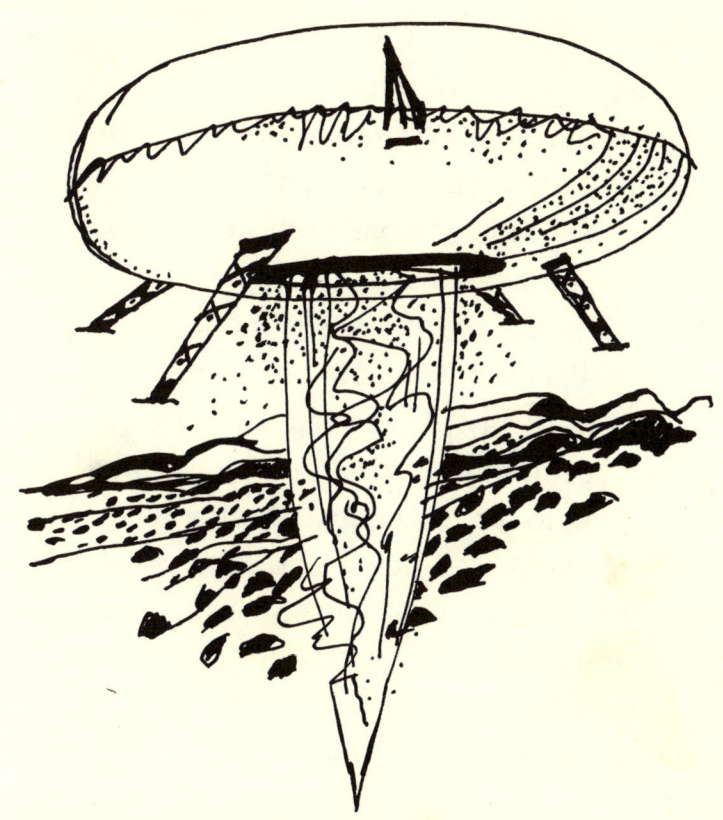

The type of "egg-shaped" craft Zamora reported he saw

before Zamora saw the craft on the ground. But the stranger never came forward to tell his own story.

Therefore, the whole case depended on what Lonnie Zamora said. Was Zamora a good and truthful witness? He had a good record as a policeman. Most people who talked to him thought he was a very honest man.

Of the many people who talked to Zamora the most important was Dr. J. Allen Hynek. Dr. Hynek was an astronomer from Northwestern University. He had been investigating UFOs for many years. On most of his investigations he worked with the Air Force. At first Dr. Hynek had doubted if UFOs were anything unusual. But by 1966 he began to change his mind. There might be something to the UFO business after all.

One of the things that helped change his mind was the Socorro, New Mexico, case. Dr. Hynek thought Zamora was telling the truth. He said Zamora saw "a physical object." But Dr. Hynek was not sure that the object was a ship from another planet. He thought Zamora might have seen a secret U.S. military craft. There was a large military base in the area. Sergeant Chavez also thought that was what Zamora saw.

The Air Force denied that it was testing any secret craft around Socorro. The Air Force said it had never tested anything that looked like what Zamora said he saw. In over ten years no evidence has ever been produced that the sighting was caused by a secret U.S. craft.

Today practically no one thinks Zamora saw a U.S. craft, or any other earthly craft, for that matter.

Did Lonnie Zamora see a spaceship? That is possible. A lot of people think that he did.

But at least one person doesn't think that he saw anything at all. That person is Philip J. Klass. Klass is an engineer and a writer. He works for the biggest aviation and space magazine in the U.S. Klass became interested in UFOs about two years after Zamora reported his sighting. Klass did not believe UFOs were spaceships. He thought that most people who reported seeing spaceships were making mistakes. What they were really seeing were planes, or balloons, or meteors, or other known objects. He thought other people were simply not telling the truth.

Klass went out to New Mexico to make his own investigation. He talked to Zamora and to Sergeant Chavez. He visited the place where the craft was supposed to have landed. Then he decided there was something wrong with Zamora's story. In fact, he thought there were many things wrong with it.

Zamora took Klass to the spot from which he said he first saw the craft and the two figures.

Klass thinks Zamora could not have seen the figures at that distance. He would have been too far away to see anything clearly.

Another thing that bothered Klass was the noise. Zamora said that he had heard a loud roar. That is what caused him to look over and see the flash of light in the first place. Zamora was then about 4,000 feet away from the place where the egg-shaped craft was supposed to have landed. But only 1,000 feet away from that spot was the home of Mr. and Mrs. Felix Phillips. Both of them were home at the time Zamora heard the roar. The windows of the house were open. But they heard nothing.

These are just two of the things Philip Klass found strange about Zamora's story. There were many others. Finally, he decided that the whole thing simply could not have happened.

But why would Zamora have made up such a story? He never tried to gain anything from it. Klass suspected that the policeman was trying to help his town. The town wanted to attract tourists. A lot of people would come to see the place where a spaceship landed.

That is Philip Klass's theory anyway. Most

A UFO photographed in McMinnville, Oregon

Ufologists do not agree with him. They think an egg-shaped spaceship really did land near Socorro, New Mexico, on April 24, 1964. They also think that Lonnie Zamora saw two men from space wearing white coveralls near the ship.

Believers and nonbelievers have been arguing about the case for years. There is no reason to think that the argument will be settled soon.

3

THE FLYING SAUCER CRASH

If spaceships from other worlds have been circling around the earth for so long, why haven't any of them crashed?

According to one story three of them actually did. Not only did the spaceships crash, they were found by the U.S. government. The occupants of the ships, according to this account, all died in the crash. They were little men from the planet Venus. The bodies of the little men and the ships themselves were taken by the U.S. government. Then the whole amazing incident was kept a secret.

The story sounds unbelievable. Here is how it began.

On March 8, 1950, a man named Silas Newton delivered a speech to a science class at the University of Denver. Newton told the story about the spaceships and the little men. Newton said he was an oil man and a millionaire. He also lectured on flying saucers. Silas Newton had been telling the same story to groups all over the country for months.

Newton said that he had learned of the crash from a friend he called "Doctor Gee." Dr. Gee, according to Newton, was "the top magnetic research specialist in the United States."

In 1949, said Newton, Dr. Gee had been working for the U.S. government. He was called in to look at a spaceship that had crashed in New Mexico. Later he was called in to examine two other spaceships that had crashed in the Southwest. A total of thirty-six small bodies were found in the wrecks.

Newton had been invited to the University of Denver by Francis F. Broman, a science teacher. Broman did not believe Newton's story. He wanted to see if his class would believe it. He gave the class five rules by which to judge the story.

1. That the report be firsthand. That is, that the

person telling the story was there when it happened.

2. That the teller show no bias or prejudice.

3. That the person who tells the story should have some expert knowledge on the subject he is talking about. In this case, Newton should know something about space travel.

4. That the facts he gives can be checked.

5. That the person telling the story be clearly identified.

After hearing Newton's story, Broman's students checked it against the five rules.

1. Newton said he heard the story from someone else, so it was not firsthand.

2. He was obviously biased in favor of the spaceship story. He would not even admit the possibility that the story might be wrong.

3. He did not know anything about space travel, or science in general. The science students found many scientific errors in his speech.

4. Since the spaceships were supposed to be hidden, there was no way of checking the facts.

5. There was also no way of finding out who the mysterious "Dr. Gee" was. Newton said he could not use the man's real name. In fact, the

A UFO photographed near Riverside, California

students had no way of finding out who Silas Newton really was.

So most of Broman's students decided that Newton's tale was not true. But a lot of other people thought it *was* true. Most of them had never heard Silas Newton speak, though.

Newspapers did hear about Newton's talk. They printed stories about it. Newton himself wrote a few articles. Then he got a friend of his named Frank Scully to write a book about the crashed spaceships and the little men. Scully didn't know anything about science, either. He had written mostly about show business. But he wrote a very lively book called *Behind the Flying Saucers.* The book was published in 1950. It was one of the first books about flying saucers. The book became very popular.

Scully's book gave many more details about the flying saucers and the little men. He said that the little men were about three-and-a-half feet tall. When doctors examined them they were found to be exactly like normal human beings except for their size. One other odd thing about them was that they all had perfect teeth. They had no cavities and no fillings.

All the little men wore the same kind of dark blue uniform with metal buttons. There did not seem to be any difference between officers and crew; they were all equal. Most of the little men carried something that looked like a timepiece. There were books and pamphlets found inside the spaceships. But no one had been able to read the language they were written in.

Dr. Gee decided that the little men came from the planet Venus. He thought that it was more likely that Venus would have life on it than the planet Mars. Besides, he thought that human beings from Mars "would probably be three or four times as large as human beings on this planet." Since the men inside the ships were smaller, not larger, he assumed they came from Venus. Just why he thought men from Mars would be large and men from Venus small, he did not explain.

Dr. Gee also said that the spaceships were powered by "the magnetic lines of force." He thought that they crashed when they ran into a "magnetic fault."

One of the crashed ships was almost 100 feet across. The second was 72 feet across. The third was only 36 feet across. The small ship had only a crew of two and must have been a scout ship. All the ships were made of a very strong metal. No scientists had ever seen metal like it before.

According to Scully's book, Dr. Gee said that

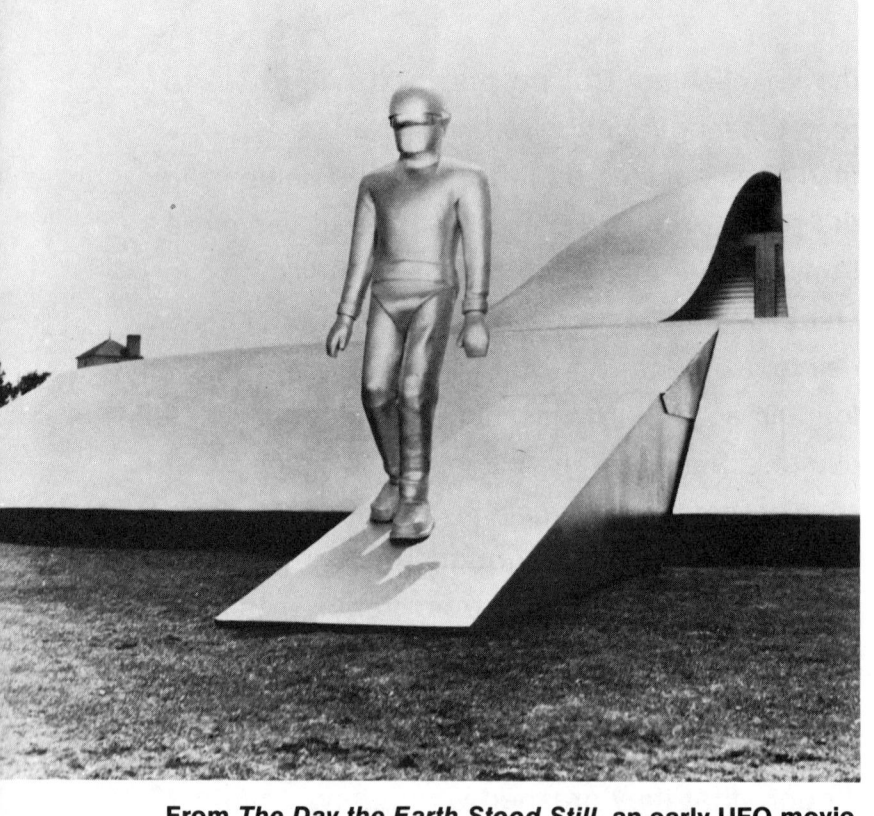

From *The Day the Earth Stood Still*, an early UFO movie

he had seen another spaceship land. But it had taken off before scientists could get close to it.

Behind the Flying Saucers reports that Dr. Gee sent all the evidence—the remains of the spaceships and everything they had in them, including the bodies of the crews—off to government laboratories. Government officials had the ships taken apart. Then all of the evidence was hidden. Dr. Gee was not allowed to test it anymore. No one he knew was allowed to look at any of it. In fact, the government denied that such evidence even existed. Government officials said they knew nothing of spaceship crashes. Dr. Gee said the government was lying. Why would the government want to keep this information secret? Dr. Gee said he didn't know why. He thought the government might be afraid that people would panic if they knew spaceships were landing.

When *Behind the Flying Saucers* came out, the government still said it did not know anything about spaceship crashes. Government officials said they had never heard of Dr. Gee, or anyone like him. They said the whole story was a hoax. But a lot of people did not believe the government. They read *Behind the Flying Saucers* and believed it. Silas Newton still wrote articles and gave lectures. But finally Silas Newton got in trouble. It turned out he was not an oil millionaire. He was trying to sell a device for finding oil. The device was worthless. Newton was arrested for fraud.

Arrested with Newton was a man named Ge-

Invading spaceships from Mars, as seen in the film, *War of the Worlds*

Bauer. GeBauer turned out to be the "mysterious Dr. Gee." He was no scientist.

The whole story had been a hoax. Everyone who had anything to do with it admits that now. But even so, the story has not gone away.

There are always rumors about the spaceships that crashed, killing all the little men inside. According to the rumors, the government is still hiding the evidence. If you ever hear these rumors just remember how they started.

4

THE NEW HAMPSHIRE KIDNAPPING

In September, 1961, Barney and Betty Hill went to Montreal, Canada, for a short vacation. On the night of September 19, they were driving back to their home in Portsmouth, New Hampshire. The drive took them down a deserted highway through the White Mountains of New Hampshire. At about ten o'clock the couple thought they saw a bright object in the sky. The object seemed to be following the car.

The Hills' dachshund Delsey became restless. Betty suggested they stop the car and walk her. While they were stopped Barney grabbed a pair of binoculars and looked at the object in the sky. He could not quite make it out.

Betty and Barney Hill

After a few minutes they began driving again. The light was still following them. Around 12 o'clock Barney stopped the car again. They were not quite sure where they were. It was somewhere near a White Mountains landmark called "the Old Man of the Mountains." Barney reached for his binoculars again. This time he could make out a shape to the light. It looked like a plane, but without wings. There were different colored lights flashing on and off. He got the feeling that somehow he was being looked at. This made him panic. He ran back to the car and drove off very quickly.

About two hours later Barney saw a road sign. He figured that he was about 35 miles from where he had last looked at the object in the sky. Neither Betty nor Barney could remember anything about the drive. They did not know why it had taken them two hours to go only 35 miles. They had "lost" two hours from their lives.

The couple did not talk much on the rest of the trip. When they got home it was daylight. They both felt very strange.

About ten days after they came back Betty began having nightmares. They were all about being kidnapped by creatures from another planet. She could not remember the dreams very well, but even after she woke up she felt scared. The dreams stopped in a week. Even so, Betty Hill continued to worry about them.

Barney did not get bad dreams. But he did feel very sick and upset. He got headaches and had trouble sleeping and felt very tired during the day. He went to see a local doctor. For a year the doctor tried to find out what was wrong with Barney. The doctor knew that something was weighing on Barney's mind, but he did not know what it was. Barney did not know either. Finally the doctor suggested that both Barney and Betty go see a specialist. The specialist was Dr. Benjamin Simon, a doctor who treated people with mental problems. Dr. Simon was an expert at hypnotizing people. When hypnotized, people sometimes remember things that they would not otherwise remember.

The Hills first saw Dr. Simon in December, 1963. They went back to see him many times. He hypnotized both of them separately. While under hypnosis they told an amazing story about what had happened to them on the night of September 19, 1961, during those "lost" hours.

According to the Hills' story, they had first been badly frightened by the sight of the thing in the sky. They were not sure quite why they had been frightened. They tried to drive away from it but got lost.

As they drove down a side road they saw flashing lights ahead. They also saw a group of figures standing by the road. The figures were signaling them to stop. Barney first thought there had been an accident and the figures were policemen. But they were not. The lights were coming from a spaceship that had landed near the road. The figures had come from the spaceship.

Barney could not remember what the figures looked like very clearly. He said they wore black jackets. One reminded him of "a red-headed Irishman." Betty's description was clearer. She said that they had strange faces with large slanting eyes and big lipless mouths.

Barney drew some pictures of what he thought the creatures looked like. The pictures were very much like the creatures Betty described. They looked like insect faces.

The eyes were what really frightened Barney. While he was hypnotized he cried out, "Ohhh, those eyes! They're in my *brain! Please,* can't I wake up?"

Barney said he was dragged into the ship. He did not struggle. He felt as though he was in sort of a dream. Betty walked to the ship. Strangely, she said she felt relaxed but frightened.

The type of creature that Barney Hill said he saw

Once in the ship the Hills were undressed. They were then examined with several different devices. They were told that they would not be hurt if they cooperated. They did cooperate and they were not hurt.

While she was describing her experience under hypnosis, Betty Hill said that after the examination she saw a "star map" on the wall of the craft. Dr. Simon told her that when she woke up she should try to draw a picture of that map. She was able to do this.

The Hills said they were released unharmed. When they got back to their car they found their dog asleep inside. They had been told by the creatures from the ship that they would not remember what had happened to them. They did not remember any of the details until they were hypnotized by Dr. Simon.

The Hills talked about their experience with many people. They even contacted some of the groups that were trying to prove that UFOs are spaceships. But they did not try to make any money off of their story. Other people who claim to have contacted creatures from UFOs have tried to make money. That makes critics of UFOs very suspicious. They think people make up the stories in order to make money or get publicity. But most of the people who talked to the Hills were convinced that they were honest, and that they really had an experience they could not explain.

Finally their story came to the attention of a writer named John Fuller. Fuller had just written an extremely popular book on UFOs. He decided to write one on the Hills' story. The book contains the actual conversations that the Hills had with Dr. Simon while they were hypnotized. Dr. Simon had tape-recorded all the sessions. They are very dramatic.

The book made the Hills famous. They ap-

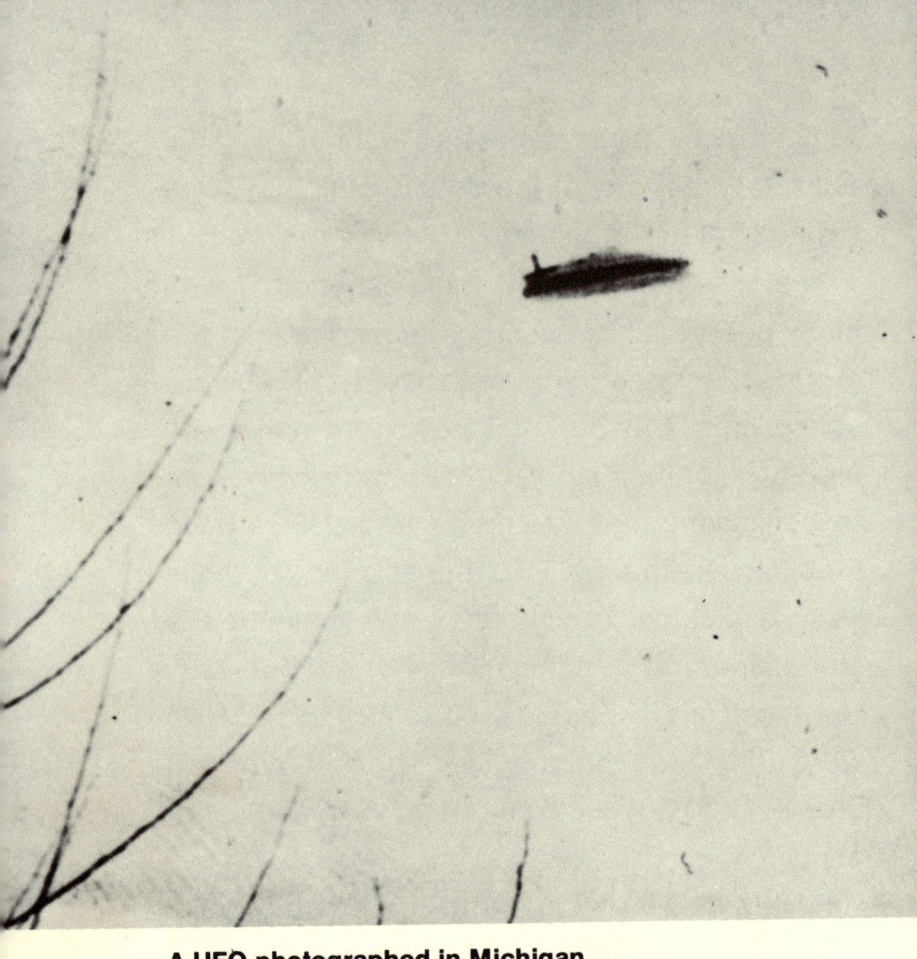

A UFO photographed in Michigan

peared on many television and radio shows. The Hill case is probably the best-known UFO case in the world today.

Barney Hill died suddenly a few years ago, but Betty Hill still appears on radio and television and at various meetings to tell her story. She says that she has not met any space people since the encounter in 1961. She does not know why the space people picked her and her husband, and she hopes they never pick her again.

But did the encounter take place as the Hills describe it? Let us look at the case a little more closely.

First, we must recognize that there is no physical evidence for the encounter. No one else in the area reported a UFO. Radar stations in New Hampshire did not track any unusual objects on the night of September 19, 1961. The only evidence we have is what the Hills said.

Most people think the Hills were honest. No one suggests they made the story up. They were telling what they thought was the truth. But did they describe what actually happened? Perhaps they did not.

The full story of the meeting with the space people only came out under hypnosis. Some people think that a hypnotized person must tell the truth. This is a myth. A hypnotized person may tell what he or she *thinks* is the truth. But it may not be what actually happened.

In fact, Dr. Simon, who hypnotized the Hills

and got the story, does not think they were taken aboard a spaceship. Yet he does not think they were lying when they told the story. How can this be?

Dr. Simon believes that the Hills really did see a bright object in the sky. They thought it was a spaceship and became frightened. After they got home Betty Hill began to have nightmares. She dreamed about being taken aboard an alien spaceship. None of that really happened, but she thought it had. Dreams can seem very real. She described her dreams to Barney. Gradually she made Barney believe them too. When they were hypnotized, both described Betty's dreams. But by that time both were convinced that what she dreamed had actually happened.

Then what happened during the two "lost" hours? That is a good question. But we are not sure there really were two "lost" hours. The Hills did not know exactly what time it was when they stopped to look at the UFO. They did get lost and drove around in the dark for a while. We do not know how long. They may just have been mistaken about the time. It is an easy sort of mistake

The spaceship *Enterprise* from the popular TV series called "Star Trek"

to make, particularly if you are scared. And the Hills were very scared.

What about the "star map" that Betty Hill drew? People who believe that the Hills were taken aboard a UFO often point to Betty Hill's star map as the best evidence. Betty's map contains twenty-six stars. Her supporters say the stars have all been identified as the kinds of stars that are likely to have planets which might contain life. Since Betty Hill knew nothing at all about astronomy, they say that she could not have made up such a map. She had to have seen it somewhere. That somewhere, they say, was inside the spaceship.

But others have looked at the "star map" and are not impressed. They point out that Betty's map does not exactly match any known star pattern. But it comes close to many patterns. There are a great many stars in the sky. The map is not very exact. By pure chance it might resemble many star clusters. In fact, the map has been identified with at least three different sets of stars.

That is where the famous Hill case stands today. Was the New Hampshire couple actually kidnapped and taken aboard a UFO? Or was the whole thing a trick of the human mind? You must make up your own mind about that.

5

THE MISSISSIPPI FISHERMEN

Nearly as famous as the Hill case is what happened in a small town in the state of Mississippi on October 11, 1973. The town is Pascagoula. On the night in question two shipyard workers named Charles Hickson and Calvin Parker were fishing from an abandoned pier in the Pascagoula River.

Neither man had a watch, so we do not know the exact time, but it was dark. The men heard a buzzing sound. Then they noticed a blue light. The light came closer and they saw it was coming from a strange-looking craft about twenty or thirty feet long. The craft came to rest thirty yards from where the men were fishing. It didn't actually land, it just hovered two or three feet above the ground.

A door suddenly appeared in the side of the craft. Three strange-looking creatures came out. They didn't walk. They floated about three feet off the ground.

The two men said the creatures were about five feet tall. They were covered with grayish, wrinkled skin. It was like "the skin of an elephant," Hickson said. The creatures didn't have real faces. Where the nose should have been there was a carrot-like growth. Two similar growths were where ears should have been. The mouth was just a hole. They didn't have any eyes.

The creatures had two arms, but no fingers. The arms ended in claw-like pincers, like the claws of a lobster. They had what looked like two legs. But the legs seemed to be stuck together. That is why they didn't seem able to walk. But since they could float they didn't need to walk.

Naturally, Hickson and Parker were terrified. "Calvin done went hysterical on me," Hickson said. They were too frightened to try and run away.

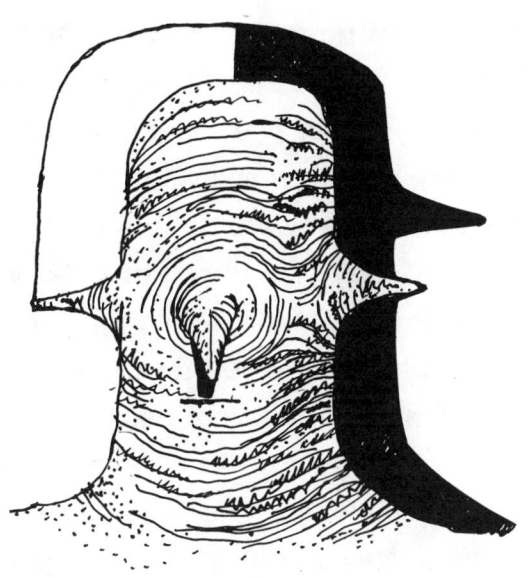

The head of the creature described by Hickson and Parker.

The creatures floated toward them. They started making buzzing noises as if they were talking to one another. Then the creatures grabbed Hickson and Parker and took them to the ship. They didn't have to drag the men, they simply floated them. Parker passed out.

The inside of the ship was brightly lighted. The creatures examined Hickson and Parker with a machine. Hickson said, "It looked like a big eye. And it went all over my body. Up and down."

The men were not hurt. But during the examination they were unable to move. After about fifteen or twenty minutes the two men were again floated out of the ship. The creatures went back inside, and the ship flew away.

Hickson and Parker were unharmed but badly shaken. At first they said they didn't know what to do. They thought they would simply forget about the whole thing. Then they decided they couldn't do that. So they went back to town.

Their first stop was the local newspaper. But the offices were closed. Then they went to the sheriff's office. News of what the two men said got around quickly. Soon all sorts of people came to Pascagoula to investigate. Charles Hickson and Calvin Parker suddenly became famous.

In many ways this case is very much like the case of Betty and Barney Hill described in the last chapter. But the Hills said that they could not remember being kidnapped. They recalled the details only after being hypnotized. The Hills also did not say very much about their case for years. Hickson and Parker said they remembered everything. They also did a great deal of talking—at least Hickson did. Parker, who was

Charles Hickson describes how he and Calvin Parker were taken aboard a UFO.

nineteen-years-old at the time, never said much. But both men did go to New York to appear on television.

What the men said got a lot of publicity. It got so much publicity that some UFO critics became very suspicious. Were Hickson and Parker just out to get publicity? Were they trying to sell the story just to make money? Hickson admitted that he needed money. He even hired a lawyer to help arrange for TV shows and other ventures for which he might be paid. But making money is no crime. The main problem was whether Hickson and Parker were telling the truth. No one could be completely sure.

Dr. J. Allen Hynek, the UFO expert, interviewed the men. He said that as far as he knew the men were telling the truth. He thought something terrifying had happened to them. But he did not say that he was sure the men had been taken aboard a UFO. Dr. Hynek was not sure what had happened.

Other Ufologists believed the story completely. But critics of UFOs were not impressed. They pointed out that Hickson and Parker had no physical evidence of their kidnapping. They also said the incident had taken place just a few blocks from the center of Pascagoula. The abandoned pier was near a busy highway. Yet no one else had reported seeing the UFO.

The whole case rested on whether the two men could be believed. And some people said that they could not be believed.

So Charles Hickson decided to take a lie de-

Scientist J. Allen Hynek thought something terrifying had happened to the two fishermen.

tector test. Parker said that he would take a lie detector test too, but he did not. Shortly after the kidnapping Parker became ill. It was reported that he had sort of a nervous breakdown because of what had happened.

Hickson also said that the kidnapping had upset him very much. But he did not report any long-lasting ill effects. He went to New Orleans to take his lie detector test, and he passed it. To many Ufologists this was positive proof that he had been telling the truth about being kidnapped by strange creatures.

But was the test positive proof? Perhaps not. Here is why. A lie detector is not 100 percent accurate. There are many cases where people have fooled lie detectors. Lie detector tests cannot be used as evidence in court. Judges know that the machines can make mistakes.

Still, lie detectors are widely used. Most experts think that they are accurate most of the time. But they are not easy to use. The person who operates the machine must be well trained at his work. A poorly trained operator is much more likely to make mistakes.

UFO critics pointed out a couple of odd things about Hickson's test. First, he went all the way to New Orleans to take the test. Mobile, Alabama, is much closer to Pascagoula than New Orleans is. There were trained lie detector operators in Mobile.

Stranger still, the lie detector operator in New Orleans was not very well trained. He was new at his work. This particular man was picked by the lawyer who was working with Hickson.

UFO critic Philip Klass offered to pay for an-

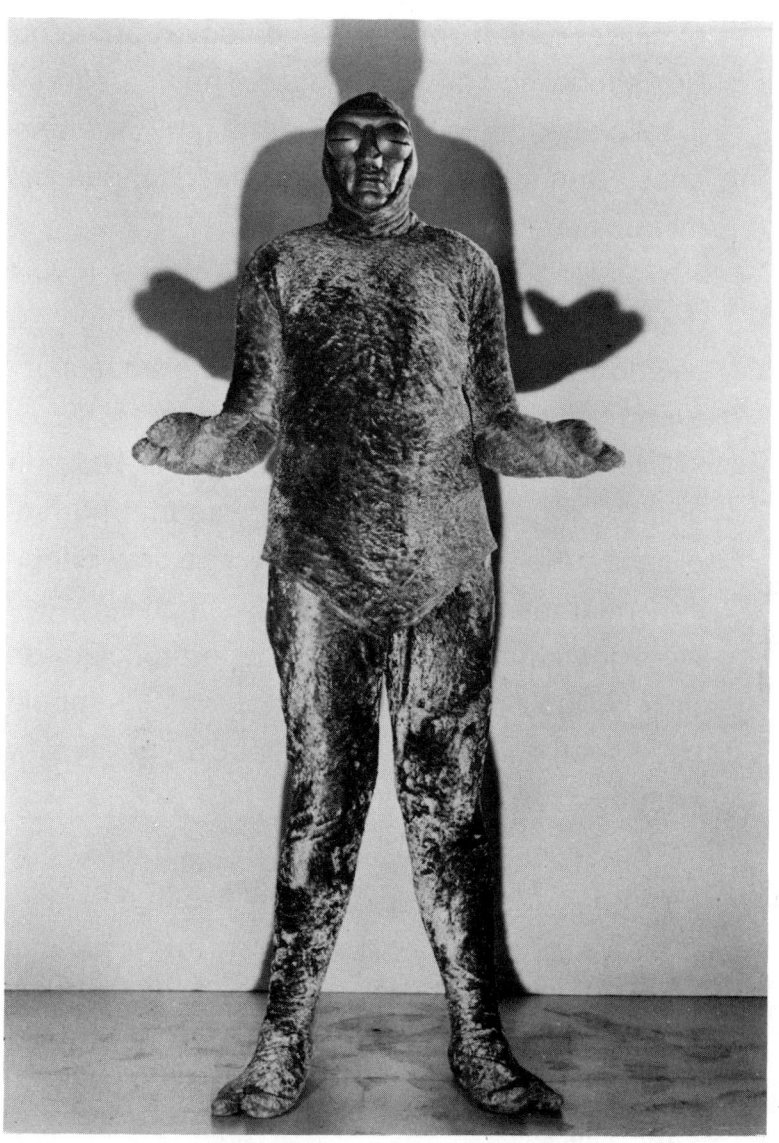

A creature from the movie, *Invaders from Mars*

other test with another lie detector operator. Hickson turned down the offer. Then he agreed to take another lie detector test at a UFO conference. But at the last minute he changed his mind.

Was Hickson telling the truth, or was his lie detector test faulty? We cannot say. Another test by another operator would answer this question. So far there has been no new test.

There were other problems with the Hickson and Parker story. The biggest was that no one else saw the spaceship. There was a drawbridge very near the place where the two men said they were kidnapped. The bridge operator was on duty at the time of the kidnapping. He should have seen a brightly lighted spaceship. He saw nothing at all.

The Pascagoula case has not been proved to be a hoax. Many people still believe that the two men were kidnapped and taken into a spaceship. But there are many unanswered questions about their story. These doubts have to be cleared up before the case can be treated seriously.

6

THE ARIZONA WOODCUTTER

We have just discussed two UFO kidnapping stories. Here is a third. At first glance it looks like the most amazing of all. This is what is supposed to have happened:

It all began on the evening of November 5, 1975. Seven young woodcutters were riding in a truck outside Heber, Arizona. They were part of a crew that had been hired to cut down trees in a national forest.

The seven men saw a UFO hovering nearby. One of the men, Travis Walton, jumped out of the truck and ran toward the object. As he got near it he was "zapped" by a beam of light. The light seemed to lift him in the air and throw him to the ground.

That sight terrified the other six. They drove off as fast as they could, leaving Walton behind. A little while later they came back to the spot to try and find their friend. He had disappeared.

They reported the disappearance to the sheriff in Heber. A search was begun. Walton could not be found. He was missing for five days.

Shortly after midnight on November 11, Travis Walton telephoned his sister, Mrs. Grant Neff. She lived in Snowflake, Arizona. Walton said he was in a phone booth in Heber, about 30 miles away. Mr. Neff and Walton's older brother Duane drove to Heber. They found Travis Walton slumped on the ground near the phone booth. He was in a confused mental state. He could remember very little of what happened after he was "zapped" by the light from the UFO.

Like the Hills, Walton was hypnotized. The hypnotist was recommended by a UFO group. Under hypnosis Walton said he was able to remember some of the details of his experience. He said that he had been knocked out by the

A creature from the science-fiction film, *This Island Earth*

beam of light. When he woke up he was inside the UFO.

He was surrounded by strange-looking creatures. They were about five feet tall. They had very large heads and big eyes. The rest of their features were very small. They did not look completely human.

Walton said he panicked at the sight of these strange beings. He hit out at one of them. When it backed off he was able to run into another room. There he met what looked like a normal human being. The figure was wearing a blue uniform and a helmet.

This being led Walton to an enormous structure. Inside he saw several disc-like craft. He also saw three other human beings, two men and a woman. They were all wearing blue coveralls and helmets. They placed a mask-like device over Walton's face. After that he claimed he remembered nothing until he woke up near the phone booth.

One of the major UFO groups became very interested in this case. So did a large national newspaper. According to stories that appeared in that newspaper, everyone involved was given a lie detector test. They all passed. It seemed as though there was very strong evidence that this fantastic case was true. But all was not as it seemed. Let us take a closer look.

The six young men who had been with Travis Walton when he disappeared were given lie detector tests. These tests were given at a time when Walton was still missing. The six were asked four questions. Three of the four questions were about whether the young woodcutters had killed or injured their companion. The aim of the test was to see if a crime had been committed. They were truthful in answering that no crime had been committed.

The fourth question was whether they saw a UFO on the day that Travis Walton disappeared. They were not asked whether Walton had been "zapped" by the UFO, or whether they thought he had been kidnapped. They all answered they had seen a UFO. According to the lie detector they were telling the truth about that.

But the lie detector is not a simple machine. It takes more than one question to determine whether or not a person is telling the truth about a subject. The men could really have seen something unidentified in the sky. It does not mean that they saw their companion get "zapped" by it.

Three months after Walton had disappeared the newspaper announced that he had taken a lie detector test and passed! Both the newspaper and the UFO group said this proved that Travis Walton had been telling the truth—that he had been kidnapped and held aboard a UFO for five days.

What the newspaper and the organization did not say was that just a few days after he returned, Walton had taken another lie detector test. He flunked this first test completely. The first test had been given by a very experienced operator. The operator said in his report that Walton's story was a hoax, and that he had never been on a spacecraft. The operator also said Walton made a deliberate attempt to fool the lie detector.

Both the organization and the newspaper knew of this first test. In fact, the newspaper had paid for the test. But no one said anything about it. These were not the sort of results they were looking for.

A saucer man attacks in the movie called *Attack of the Saucer Men*.

Later, a much less-experienced operator was found. When he gave Walton a test the young man passed with flying colors. The results of this test were given wide publicity. But when other lie detector experts examined the report of the test they were very critical. They did not think the test had been given correctly. They said the results should not be counted. As we mentioned earlier, the lie detector is not a perfect machine. A great deal depends on the skill of the person who is operating the machine.

UFO critic Philip Klass found out about the original Travis Walton lie detector test. He also found out some other things about the young man who said he had been kidnapped by creatures from a UFO.

Walton had once been in trouble with the law for forging checks. Walton also had a long-standing interest in UFOs. His friends called him a "UFO freak." He often said that he wanted to contact a UFO. His older brother Duane was also interested in UFOs. Travis said if he was ever picked up by a UFO he would try to convince the occupants to go back and get Duane, his brother, so they could share the experience.

In addition, Klass pointed out that during the five days that Travis Walton was missing his family did not seem the least bit worried about him. Duane kept saying that he was sure Travis had not been harmed. He also said he thought Travis would be returned to about the same spot from which he had disappeared.

Klass concluded that Travis Walton's story

UFO skeptic Philip Klass talks to a reporter.

about being kidnapped and taken aboard a UFO was a hoax. A lot of people who are interested in UFOs don't agree with Philip Klass very often. A lot of them don't even like him very much. But many of them agreed that the Walton case was a hoax. Some had come to that conclusion even before the results of the first lie detector test were revealed.

The next time you hear a really sensational UFO tale, remember the Travis Walton case. That sounded sensational too—at first.

7
MOTHMAN

On the night of November 15, 1966, two young couples from the little town of Point Pleasant, West Virginia, decided to take a drive. They drove to what was called "the Old TNT Area." That was the name given to an ammunition dump that had not been used for years. The dump was about seven miles from Point Pleasant.

The road to the TNT area was dark and deserted. As their car passed an abandoned power plant, the two couples saw a figure standing at the side of the road. It was a very weird-looking figure.

"It was shaped like a man, but bigger," said one of the boys. "Maybe six-and-a-half or seven feet tall. And it had big wings folded against its back."

The thing was staring at them. "It was those eyes that got us," said one of the girls. "It had two big red eyes, like automobile reflectors."

They stopped the car and looked at it. "For a minute we could only stare at it," said the boy. "Then it just turned and sort of shuffled toward the open door of the old power plant. We didn't wait around."

They certainly didn't. The driver swung the car around and headed back toward town. He pressed the gas pedal to the floor. He figured the car must have hit 100 miles per hour. But he didn't bother to look at the speedometer. He was too scared. The thing was following them.

It was flying right over the car. No matter how fast they went, it kept up. It didn't seem to flap its wings. It just glided along, but very fast. And it made a noise. "It squeaked. . .like a big mouse," said one of the girls. The young people guessed that when the thing spread its wings out they measured about 10 feet from tip to tip.

The thing followed them right to the city limits. Then it turned off and disappeared. The terrified teenagers went right to the local sheriff. The sheriff didn't know what to make of the story. He decided to drive out to the Old TNT Area and check it out. He found no trace of the winged thing.

Word of this very strange encounter got around quickly. Soon newspaper, radio, and television reporters arrived. They began asking the four teenagers a lot of questions. The story was carried in newspapers and on radio and television all over the country.

Now about this time you may be saying, "That's a strange story all right, but what does it have to do with UFOs?" That's a good question. I don't have a really good answer.

Before November 16, 1966, a number of UFOs had been reported in the area of Point Pleasant. For years there had been a large number of UFO sightings reported in West Virginia. People just seem to have assumed that the winged creature came from a UFO. No one ever actually saw it flying out of a spaceship. But the connection has stuck. Everyone who believes in the creature also believes that it has something to do with UFOs.

The two couples who first saw the thing called it "the Bird." That's what it looked like to them. But a reporter named the creature "Mothman." The thing didn't look like a moth. But Mothman was a nice catchy name. Like the UFO connection, the name has stuck, for no really good reason.

The encounter of November 15 was only the beginning. The next night a group of people drove out to visit the Ralph Thomas family. The visitors were a man, two women, and a small child. The Thomas family was one of the few that lived near the Old TNT Area. The people parked in front of the Thomas house and got out of the car. Then something rose up near the car.

"It seemed as if it had been lying down," one of the women told Ufologist John Keel. "It rose up slowly from the ground. A big gray thing. Bigger than a man, with terrible glowing eyes."

The woman was stunned. It was almost as if she was in a trance. She actually dropped the child she was carrying in her arms. Then she recovered. She picked up the child. Then everyone ran for the house. Mr. and Mrs. Thomas were not at home, but their children were. The visitors and the young Thomases locked the door and all the windows.

Mothman shuffled up onto the porch and looked in the window. One of the visitors phoned the sheriff. By the time he arrived the creature was gone.

One of the women in the group was so frightened she had nightmares. She kept thinking she saw the monster near her home. Finally she had to see a doctor. It was many months before she was able to sleep peacefully again.

On November 25, Thomas Ury was driving near the Old TNT Area. It was early morning. He saw what looked like a tall man in a gray coat standing in a field near the road. Suddenly the "man" spread his wings, and took off. According to Ury, the thing went "straight up, like a helicopter."

It started circling around the car. Ury said he was going at least 70 miles an hour. But the thing kept up with him. Ury was driving a convertible. He was afraid the thing would come right

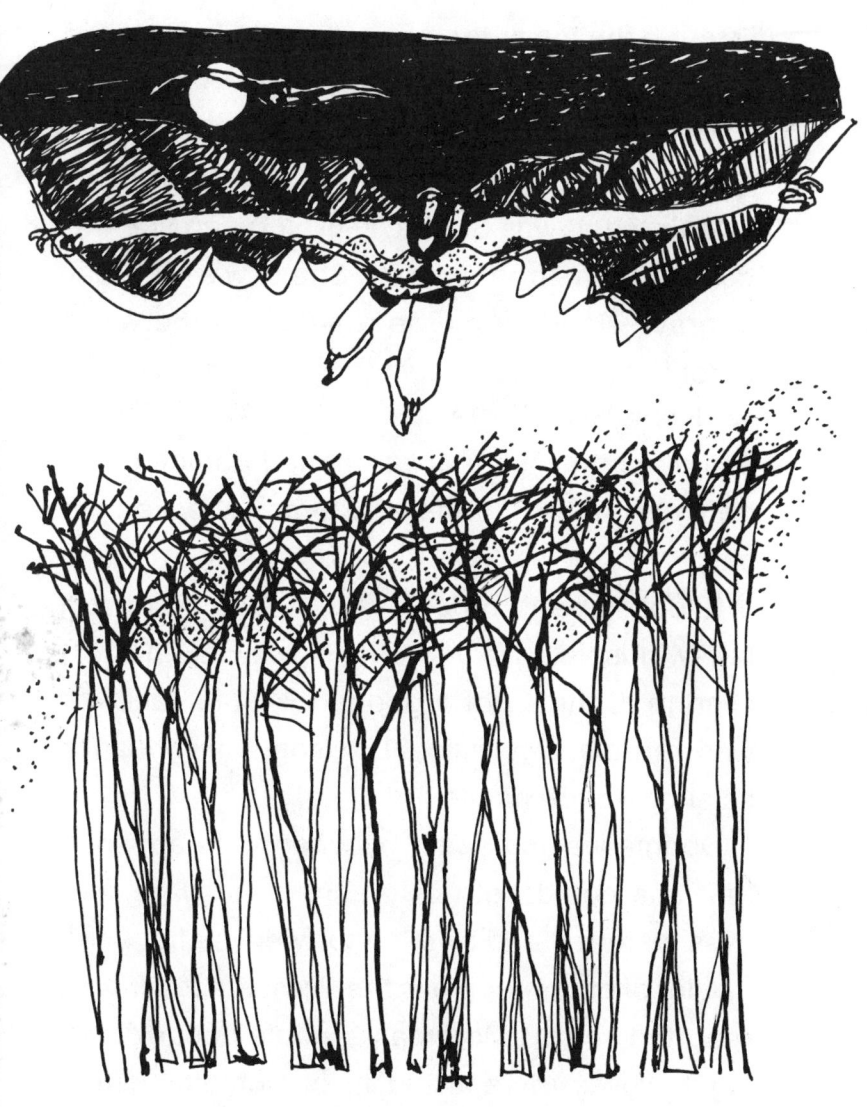

Mothman, the winged creature that flies

through the top of the car and grab him. Instead, it just flew away.

Two days later an eighteen-year-old girl named Connie Carpenter was driving in the same area. It was Sunday morning and she was coming home from church. She saw a "tall man in gray" standing by the road. Then the wings unfolded. Mothman flew straight for her car.

"Those eyes!" she said. "They were very red and once they were fixed on me I couldn't take my eyes off them." She very nearly wrecked her car.

It looked as if the creature was going to ram her windshield. It veered off only at the last second. Connie got a good look at its face. "It was horrible," she said. "Like something out of a science-fiction movie."

Connie was so upset by what had happened that she could not go to school for days. Her eyes were red and swollen for weeks afterward.

A lot of other people in the Point Pleasant area reported seeing Mothman. People in surrounding towns also reported it, or something that looked like it. Soon people all over West Virginia and beyond said they had seen it.

The wreckage of the Silver Bridge near Point Pleasant

Mothman sightings were reported for over a year. Then on December 15, 1967, almost thirteen months after the first sighting, something terrible happened. The Silver Bridge which crossed the Ohio River near Point Pleasant collapsed. The collapse took place at the height of the rush hour. Forty-six vehicles plunged into the river. Many people were killed. This was a major disaster.

The bridge was old. It had been built in 1928. It could not stand up to the heavy traffic of the 1960s. Engineers said the bridge collapse was a tragedy, but that there was nothing unusual about it. People who believed in Mothman thought differently. Somehow—no one was sure how—Mothman and the collapse of the Silver Bridge were connected. In any case, Mothman sightings dropped off after the bridge collapse.

What was Mothman? Today no one can say for sure. But there are many theories.

A biologist from West Virginia University said Mothman might be a real bird. He suggested that what people saw was a sandhill crane. The sandhill crane is very large. It can stand six feet tall. The bird also has red patches under its eyes. Everyone said Mothman had big red eyes.

The sandhill crane is a very rare bird. It does not live in West Virginia. But the biologist suggested that one might have wandered in. People seeing one of these large birds for the first time could be frightened and confused. They might think it was a creature from outer space.

There is a wildlife preserve near the Old TNT Area. The rangers in the preserve did not report

Scene from the early flying saucer movie, *The Thing from Another World*. The monster in this film was a killer plant.

seeing any strange birds. Certainly they saw nothing like a sandhill crane. They thought that if such a bird had been in the area they would have seen it. They would also have known it was a bird, not a monster.

Other people suggested other kinds of birds. Someone thought it might be a large owl.

But those who said they saw Mothman would not accept any bird suggestions. They said that if the scientists had seen what they saw, they would stop talking about birds.

Other people thought the whole thing started as a joke. Then the joke got out of hand. There was so much publicity, people became convinced that the story was true. Then they began to think that they saw Mothman themselves. That is what is known as "mass hysteria." Mass hysteria is what most scientists today believe was behind the Mothman scare.

But to the people who said they saw Mothman, that explanation is even worse than the sandhill crane. They are sure they saw some sort of creature from outer space.

We may believe the stories about Mothman or we may not believe them. But in order for scientists to accept them, they need evidence. At least they need a picture of Mothman. Best of all, they need Mothman itself. So far they have nothing but the stories. The stories alone are not good enough. At one time a lot of people reported seeing a unicorn. Today we know there is no such thing as a unicorn.

8
THE MYSTERIOUS MEN IN BLACK

Some people who have seen UFOs get very frightened. They are afraid that one day they may be visited by the mysterious Men in Black. The Men in Black, or MIBs, will try to make them stop talking about UFOs. The MIBs may use threats or they may use force. No one wants to meet them.

The idea that there are mysterious Men in Black who go around trying to silence people interested in UFOs goes back to 1953. It began with a man named Albert Bender. Bender was the head of a small organization of UFO buffs—people interested in UFOs. The organization had a very grand title. It was called the International Flying Saucer Bureau (IFSB). But it only had a few hundred members and it wasn't international. Bender also put out a little publication called *Space Review.* It contained news about UFOs and about people who were interested in UFOs. There were many other groups like the IFSB and magazines like *Space Review.*

Interest in UFOs was growing and things seemed to be going well for Bender's group and the publication. But the October, 1953, issue of *Space Review* contained two startling notices.

The first notice said that IFSB had learned that the flying saucer mystery was nearly solved. However, the solution could not yet be revealed.

The second notice, in the very same issue, was even more astounding. It said that the flying saucer mystery had actually been solved! The solution, however, was being kept secret on "orders from a higher source."

The notice sounded as if it would be dangerous to reveal the "solution." It ended with this scary warning: "We advise those engaged in saucer work to please be very cautious."

That was the last issue of *Space Review.*

The Men in Black, or MIBs

Bender stopped the publication, and dissolved the International Flying Saucer Bureau. Albert Bender's friends who were interested in UFOs were shocked. They could not imagine what caused him to act this way. At first, Bender refused to say any more. He just acted very strangely. He acted scared.

Finally he did tell an odd tale, or part of one anyway. He said that before he stopped publishing *Space Review* he had been visited by three men in dark suits. (Later he said they wore black suits. That is where the name "Men in Black" comes from). Bender said they "ordered" him to stop publishing. He said that they had been "pretty rough" and that he had been "scared to death." After their visit he "actually couldn't eat for a couple of days."

Who were these Men in Black? Why were they after Albert Bender? What did he know that they wanted kept quiet? Bender refused to answer any of those questions. In fact, for almost ten years he wouldn't say anything more about the subject.

Not all of Albert Bender's friends believed his story about the three men. Some of them said that Bender's publication and organization were running out of money and that was why he had to close them down. The story about the three men, they said, was just an excuse. It made the failure of the IFSB and *Space Review* sound exciting.

But a lot of people interested in UFOs did believe Albert Bender's story about the Men in Black. At least they thought it *might* be true. They wondered who the Men in Black could be.

Bender's story made it sound as if they were some sort of government agents. Perhaps they were from the FBI or the CIA, or special agents from the Air Force. The Air Force was supposed to be investigating UFOs. At that time many UFO buffs thought the Air Force was hiding important information about UFOs. But after a few years the popularity of that explanation began to fade. There was another and more interesting explanation. The Men in Black were not agents of the government—not an earthly government anyway. The Men in Black themselves were creatures from another planet!

In 1963, over ten years after meeting the Men in Black, Albert Bender said, yes, it's true the MIBs are from another planet. Bender wrote a book called *Flying Saucers and the Three Men in Black.* In the book Bender described other meetings he had with the Men in Black. He also told of meeting "three beautiful women dressed in tight white uniforms." Both the Men in Black and the Women in White had "glowing eyes."

Flying Saucers and the Three Men in Black is a very strange book. Not many people have ever read it. Not many people have even heard of it.

There is no evidence that anything in the book is true. But none of this made any difference as far as the story of the MIBs was concerned. By that time a lot of other people began reporting them. Albert Bender, who started the whole thing, had almost been forgotten.

A typical MIB story goes something like this. A person sees a UFO and takes a picture of it. A few days later he is visited by a man or group of men wearing black suits. The men have black hair and dark complexions. Sometimes they wear dark glasses. They look strange. The men arrive in a large black car, usually a brand-new shiny Cadillac.

They tell the UFO witness that they are from the government or the Air Force. They may pull out some sort of official-looking card. But they don't let anyone examine the card closely. They ask the witness all sorts of questions. They tell him that the government thinks that he should not talk about what he has seen. Then they take the negative of his photograph. They say they will return it in a few days. They are never heard from again.

Sometimes the Men in Black make threats. A

Photographs of a UFO taken by a California highway inspector. He later said that the original prints were carried off by a mysterious man who said he was an Air Force officer.

visit with them can be very upsetting. Witnesses have reported becoming quite sick after the MIBs paid a call.

But each case is different. Let's look first at the case of Rex Heflin. Heflin was a highway inspector for the state of California. On August 3, 1965, Heflin said he saw a UFO. He was sitting in his parked car near the Santa Ana Freeway. He also happened to have a Polaroid camera with him and snapped a series of pictures. The pictures show an object that looks like an old-fashioned straw hat floating above the ground.

Heflin's pictures are very clear. They were printed in magazines and newspapers all over the country. In 1967 a scientific committee from the University of Colorado was investigating UFOs. They wanted to know more about Heflin's pictures. Since the pictures were made with a Polaroid camera there were no negatives. But the investigators thought they could learn something from the original prints. They would be clearer than any copies.

Heflin said that he did not have the original prints anymore. He said he had already given them to a man from the Air Force. The Air Force insisted that it had never sent anyone to take the prints. The prints were never located.

On October 11, 1967, after he told his story to the investigators from the University of Colorado, Heflin claimed that he got another strange visit. A man who said he was Captain C.H. Edmonds of the Air Force came to interview Heflin. He asked Heflin if he wanted his photos back. Heflin said no, and Captain Edmonds was "visibly relieved." Then Captain Edmonds began talking about all sorts of strange subjects like the Bermuda Triangle. The Bermuda Triangle is a place in the ocean near the island of Bermuda. Planes and ships are supposed to disappear mysteriously there.

While Captain Edmonds was talking, Heflin looked out his window. He saw a large dark car parked in the street. It had some sort of lettering on the door but he could not make it out. There was a man in the back seat. The man seemed to be working some sort of machine that gave off a violet glow. Heflin thought his conversation was being recorded. During the interview Heflin's radio began making strange sounds.

When investigators tried to locate Captain

C.H. Edmonds of the Air Force they found that there was no such person.

Stan Gordon, the head of a Pennsylvania UFO group, reported a more violent brush with one of the Men in Black in 1973. A woman in Pennsylvania said she had seen a space creature with big feet walking outside her trailer home. Gordon and a couple of others went to investigate. They were taking photographs of the footprints when a man in a black suit drove up in a station wagon.

The man jumped out of the car and started asking a lot of questions. When he found out that the footprints had been photographed, he grabbed the camera and tore the film out of it. Then he destroyed the footprints and drove away—fast.

Dr. J. Allen Hynek, the astronomer who has been investigating UFOs for many years, has traveled all over the world to talk to people who have claimed they saw UFOs. Dr. Hynek has never seen a MIB, but he has certainly heard about them.

Scientist Edward U. Condon and President Lyndon Johnson. Condon headed a scientific committee which studied UFOs.

In June, 1974, Dr. Hynek went to Mexico. He wanted to talk to Carlos Antonio de los Santos Monteil, a young pilot. Monteil said he had seen three UFOs during a flight to Mexico City.

Dr. Hynek talked to the pilot for two hours. He then arranged to meet him the next morning at breakfast to continue the talk. But Monteil did not show up for breakfast.

Later, a friend of Monteil's told Dr. Hynek that the pilot had been "silenced" by the Men in Black. According to Monteil's friend, the pilot had been driving home after the first interview when a car forced him off the road. Two men jumped out of the car and began shouting at Monteil. They warned him to keep his mouth shut about UFOs—or else. The pilot decided that it would not be wise to say any more. That is why he did not appear for the breakfast meeting.

Stanton Friedman, who gives UFO lectures, says the Men in Black contacted him after he gave a lecture in Oklahoma City. Three of them took him to lunch. They asked him a lot of questions about UFOs. After lunch they drove him home in their shiny black Cadillac. Friedman says he never saw them again.

Perhaps the strangest MIB story of all was told by the writer Ivan Sanderson. Sanderson did not give any names or dates. This is what he said happened:

Several members of a family saw a UFO. A few weeks later they were visited by a very strange-

Ivan Sanderson, who told a very strange story about a Man in Black

looking person. This person was about seven feet tall, had a very small head, and thin legs and arms. His skin was very white.

It was bitterly cold outside. The strange visitor was wearing a fur hat, but only a light jacket. He took out an official-looking card. But no one got a close look at it. He was also wearing a badge. He took the badge off when people began trying to take a close look at it.

The tall man said that he worked for an insurance company. He hinted that the family had inherited a lot of money. However, he would not give any details.

When the man sat down he pulled up the leg of his pants a bit. The eldest daughter in the family saw a green wire. It ran out of the top of the man's sock and into his flesh.

The family lived out in the country. After the interview was over the tall man walked out of the house. A large black car came down a dirt road leading from the woods. Two people were in the car. It stopped in front of the house and the tall man got in. The car then drove off. Though it was pitch dark, the driver never turned the headlights on.

Who are the mysterious Men in Black? Do they exist at all? A lot of people think that they do not. No one has ever produced any evidence that they exist. All we have are stories. Often the Men in Black seem to serve as an excuse. If someone does not want to, or cannot, produce a picture of a UFO he says the Men in Black took it. If someone does not want to be questioned too closely about what he saw or what he is doing, he says the Men in Black have "silenced" him.

But whatever they are, or are not, a lot of people have reported seeing the Men in Black. A lot more people are afraid of them. They have become a permanent part of UFO lore.

9
CLOSE ENCOUNTERS IN OTHER LANDS

The terms "flying saucer" and "unidentified flying object" were first coined in the United States. The United States has always been the center of UFO activity. But UFOs have been reported all over the world. So have encounters with occupants of the UFOs. Here are some well-known cases from other countries.

One of the early UFO classic sightings took place on the island of New Guinea near Australia. The report came from a remote mission station at the village of Boianai.

The Reverend Norman E.G. Cruttwell, who

headed the Anglican missions in that area, was very interested in UFOs in the 1950s. He had collected many sighting reports. He asked all his missionaries to send him accounts of sightings. He received plenty of them. The most spectacular was the one that he got from Rev. William Gill, describing what happened on the evenings of June 26 and June 27, 1959.

At about 6:45 P.M. on June 26, a bright light was sighted in the sky. The mission workers called Rev. Gill. The light turned out to be coming from a large disc-like craft. After watching the thing for about fifteen minutes, Rev. Gill saw several "glowing" men in it. They were moving around, but he could not tell what they were doing. Two other small craft also appeared. They darted around the sky, coming in and out of view. The large ship hovered in one place. Rev. Gill called it "the Mother Ship." All in all, the ships were in sight for about four hours.

The next evening, shortly after sunset, the ships were back. This time Rev. Gill could see the figures on the big ship more clearly. "We watched the figures appear on top [of the UFO]—four of them—there is no doubt that they were human. This is possibly the same object I took to be the 'Mother Ship' last night. Two smaller UFOs were seen at the same time, stationary, one above the hills west, and another overhead." As on the previous night, the figures seemed to "glow."

Rev. Gill wrote, "On the large one [UFO], two of the figures seemed to be doing something near the center of the deck." They were bending over and raising their arms. One of the figures was looking down at the group on the ground. Rev. Gill waved to the figure in the UFO. To his surprise the figure waved back. One of the other people on the ground waved both his arms over his head. Two of the figures on the UFO did the same.

Said Rev. Gill, "There seemed to be no doubt that our movements were answered."

Rev. Gill then got a flashlight. He blinked it on and off in the direction of the UFO. As if to answer, the UFO moved back and forth.

After a few minutes the figures on the UFO lost interest in what was happening on the ground. They disappeared from the deck. They reappeared at 6:25 and a blue spotlight came on under the craft.

The type of UFO reported by Rev. William Gill

Then a very odd thing happened—not on the UFO, but on the ground. Rev. Gill and all of those with him went inside for dinner. Rev. Gill and the others seemed to be on the verge of being the first people on earth to meet visitors from outer space. But they broke off their observations to eat. This action is almost unbelievable. Rev. Gill has never been able to explain why he did this.

All he has said was that it was his habit to eat at that time. This has led UFO critics to say there is something fishy about the whole story.

In any event, when he came out from dinner a half hour later the large UFO was still there. But now it seemed farther away. The crew was no longer to be seen. Then everyone on the ground went to evening services. When they came out again at 7:45 the UFO was gone.

The following evening a total of eight UFOs were spotted in the same area. But they did not get close and no figures were seen.

A report of this remarkable sighting was signed by Rev. Gill and twenty-five native witnesses. The report was then sent to Rev. Cruttwell who made it public.

This case has been difficult to investigate. New Guinea is far from places where there are scientists able to make such an investigation. The mission station where the sighting was made is deep in the jungle. The natives who said they saw the UFO have not been interviewed by outside investigators. The entire case really must rest on the testimony of Rev. Gill. From all accounts he is a respected and trustworthy churchman. Did he really see a spaceship? Did he wave to the visitors from outer space, and then go to dinner? Make up your own mind about this one.

Ventura Maceiras lived in the small town of Tres Arroyos, Argentina. He was seventy-three years old and worked as a night watchman. At about 10:30 in the evening of December 30, 1972, Maceiras was listening to his radio outside of the shack in which he lived. Suddenly his radio began to fail. He hit it a few times but it didn't get any better, so he turned it off. Then he heard a loud humming sound coming from above.

Maceiras looked up and saw a bright light above the trees. In the middle of the light was some sort of ship. The color of the ship kept changing from orange to purple. Maceiras could see it had a cabin with windows. Through the windows he could see two figures. The figures wore helmets. They also wore what looked like some kind of space suits. The suits seemed to be made up of inflated tubes joined together. The figures were gazing right at Maceiras through slanting eyes. Their mouths were only thin lines.

The craft drew closer. Maceiras could see

The creature that Ventura Maceiras said he saw

instruments and dials glowing inside the cabin. Suddenly a bright light shot out from the bottom of the craft. It blinded the old man for a moment. The humming noise got louder, and the craft rose and disappeared.

The next day Maceiras became sick. The sickness lasted for weeks. He suffered from headaches and stomachaches. His hair fell out. His eyes were swollen and watering and he had trouble speaking.

After a few weeks the unpleasant symptoms went away. Then a most remarkable thing happened. Seventy-three-year-old Ventura Maceiras began growing a new set of teeth—his third.

On September 3, 1967, Paula Valdez of Caracas, Venezuela, came home from work with a bad headache. She took some aspirins and went to bed. She turned on her radio and dozed off. She was asleep only a short time when she was awakened by a whistling sound. First she thought there was something wrong with the radio. She began twisting the dials. Then she realized she was no longer alone in her room.

There was a small man-like creature leaning over her. It had a large head and bulging eyes. It said to her, "I want you to come with us so that you will know other worlds. You will realize how small your world is."

If this statement was meant to calm her, it failed. Paula Valdez began screaming. The little man then sort of floated out of the room. But Paula kept screaming until her family came. None of them saw the creature.

On the 8th of September, 1967, another young woman in Caracas had a very similar experience. Alicia Rivas was just going to bed when she saw a strange creature outside her bedroom window. It looked like a small man, but she didn't look too closely. She was far too frightened. She just closed her eyes and started screaming. Her relatives rushed into the room. They saw a little man surrounded by a bluish-green light floating away over the rooftops. Alicia's brother-in-law got the best look. He said the little man seemed to be wearing silvery clothing.

At five the next morning another flying man was reported in another part of Venezuela. Officer Porfirio Antonio Andrade of the city of Valencia was on guard in city hall. He heard a strange buzzing noise outside. He went out to investigate.

On the front steps of city hall he saw a little man about four feet tall. The man had a large head and bulging eyes which glowed red. He was also wearing a silver uniform.

Officer Andrade pulled out his gun and pointed it at the creature. Then he heard a voice come from above. It said, "Don't do him any harm. We are here on a peaceful mission. He'll do you no harm."

The voice was coming from a disc-like craft

that was hovering overhead. The little man on the ground then began talking. He repeated he meant no harm. Then he said that "they" wanted Andrade to come with them to a distant world. The creature said there would be many advantages on this world for Earthmen.

Andrade was badly frightened. He didn't want to go anywhere. He told the little man he couldn't leave because he was on duty. The little man then just flew up to the object hovering overhead. A door opened in the side of the disc and the little man sailed in. Then there was a noise and a jet of flame from the disc and the object flew away.

Here are three Canadian cases. The first comes from the city of Ottawa.

On an evening in August, 1965, a man named Harris and his girlfriend went for a drive. At about 9 P.M. they parked near a reservoir outside the city. They saw a very bright light appear in the sky. They saw the light was coming from a round craft of some sort. The craft stopped and hovered about fifteen or twenty feet above the water. A sliding door opened in the side of the craft and a figure appeared. It was shortly joined by two other figures. The craft was too far away for Harris to make out any details of the figures, but they looked human. The girl became frightened. Harris drove off while the ship was still hovering over the reservoir.

There were several other cars in the area. But as far as is known no one else reported anything unusual.

On June 13, 1967, a mine worker from Caledonia in the province of Ontario had a very strange experience. Carmen Cuneo stepped outside the mine in which he was working. He saw two craft hovering about twelve feet above the ground. One of the craft was cigar-shaped and over 30 feet long. The other was disc-shaped. It was about 15 feet in diameter.

There were three little men outside of the cigar-shaped object. The little men were wearing helmets like those worn by miners. The helmets had amber lights on top. Cuneo watched this scene for several minutes. Then he decided he had better find another witness.

He went into the mine and called out his friend, Merv Hannigan. The three little men had disap-

The movie *Star Wars* is one of the most popular ever made. It shows our fascination with creatures from space.

peared before Hannigan could see them. But the UFOs were still there. The two men watched the two UFOs for about twenty minutes. Then the two craft took off in a blaze of flashing lights.

On June 9, 1971, Esther Clapperson of Rosedale, Alberta, Canada, saw a bright light outside her house. She went out on the front porch with her dog. She was surprised to see a large rectangular object on the road nearby.

Then she saw three men. Two were inside the craft. She could see them through a window. The third was outside. The outside man seemed to be trying to attract the attention of the men inside. Mrs. Clapperson said that the faces of the three were covered. They were about five feet tall and wore dull green clothing. She also noticed they had very strange-looking hands. "They were like mittens," she said. The thumbs were big and pointed. The hands were rather claw-like.

Mrs. Clapperson said she wanted to get a closer look. But her dog stopped her. The animal was shaking badly. It kept trying to push her back into the house. She thought the dog might sense some danger, so she went back inside. She was going to tell her brother to take a look. But when she glanced out the window the ship and the three men were gone. She had just been inside for a few seconds. She had no idea what had happened.

This is only a sample, a very small sample, of hundreds and hundreds of reports that have been received from around the world. I'm sure you will agree they are sensational. But are they true? Do they describe things that really happened? Or did people dream these encounters, or make them up altogether? We cannot say for sure. None of these cases has been thoroughly investigated. As we have seen, investigations often show things did not happen as they are reported to have happened. Investigations have often shown a story to be a hoax.

So we must treat these stories with care. But that should not keep us from enjoying them. It is quite thrilling to think that one day we may look out our window and see a UFO. Then slowly a door in the UFO opens, and three little men float out. . .

INDEX

Air Force, U.S., 26, 85-90
Andrade, Porfirio Antonio, 104-105
Argentina, 101-103
Arizona, 61-69
Arnold, Kenneth, 15
Attack of the Saucer Men (movie), 67

Behind the Flying Saucers (Scully), 34-37
Bender, Albert, 81-86
Bermuda Triangle, 89
Boianai, New Guinea, 96
Broman, Francis F., 31, 32, 33

Caledonia, Canada, 108
California, 88-90
Canada, 105-109
Caracas, Venezuela, 103
Carpenter, Connie, 76
Chavez, Sam, 22, 23, 26, 27
Clapperson, Esther, 108
Close Encounters of the First Kind, 16
Close Encounters of the Second Kind, 16
Close Encounters of the Third Kind, 16
Close Encounters of the Third Kind (movie), 16, 17, 18
Colorado, University of, 88, 89
Condon, Edward U., 91
Cruttwell, Rev. Norman E. G., 96, 100
Cuneo, Carmen, 106, 108

Day the Earth Stood Still, The (movie), 36
Denver, University of, 31

Edmonds, Captain C. H., 89-90
Eilbes, Mr. and Mrs. Peter, 12-13
Enterprise ("Star Trek" spaceship), 49

Flatwoods, West Virginia, 9
Flatwoods Monster, 10

Flying Saucers and the Three Men in Black (Bender), 85-86
Friedman, Stanton, 92
Fuller, John, 45

GeBauer, Mr. (Dr. Gee), 31, 32, 35-38
Gill, Rev. William, 97-101
Gordon, Stan, 90

Hannigan, Merv, 106, 108
Harris, Mr. (Ottawa, Canada), 105
Heber, Arizona, 61-69
Heflin, Rex, 88-89
Hickson, Charles, 51-60
Hill, Barney and Betty, 39-50, 51, 54, 62
Hynek, Dr. J. Allen, 26, 56, 57, 90-92

International Flying Saucer Bureau, 82-84
Invaders from Mars (movie), 59

Johnson, President Lyndon, 91

Keel, John, 73
Klass, Philip J., 27-29, 58, 68-69

Lie detectors, 56-58, 60, 65-69

Maceiras, Ventura, 101-103
Mars, 35, 38, 59
McMinnville, Oregon, UFO photographed in, 29
Men in Black, 81-95

Mexico, 91
Michigan, UFO photographed in, 46
Milwaukee, Wisconsin, 12
Mississippi, 51-60
Monteil, Carlos Antonio de los Santos, 91-92
Mothman, 70-80

Neff, Mr. and Mrs. Grant, 62
New Guinea, 96-101
New Hampshire, 39-50
Newton, Silas, 31-38

Oklahoma City, Oklahoma, 92
Ontario (Canada), 106
Ottawa, Canada, 105

Parker, Calvin, 51-60
Pascagoula, Mississippi, 51-60
Pennsylvania, 90
Phillips, Mr. and Mrs. Felix, 28
Point Pleasant, West Virginia, 70-80
Poland Springs, Maine, 10

Rivas, Alicia, 103-104
Riverside, California, UFO photographed in, 33
Rosedale, Alberta, Canada, 108

Sanderson, Ivan, 92-94
Scully, Frank, 34, 35
Silver Bridge, collapse of, 77-78
Simon, Dr. Benjamin, 42, 44, 45, 47-48
Socorro, New Mexico, UFO landing, 20-29

111

Space Review, 82-84
"Star Trek," 49
Star Wars, 107

Thing from Another World, The (movie), 79
This Island Earth (movie), 63
Thomas, Ralph, and family, 73-74
Tres Arroyos, Argentina, 101-103

Ufologists, 15, 24, 29, 56, 57, 73
Ury, Thomas, 74

Valdez, Paula, 103
Valencia, Venezuela, 104
Venezuela, 103-105
Venus (planet), men from, 30, 35

Walton, Duane, 62, 68
Walton, Travis, 61-69
War of the Worlds (movie), 38
West Virginia, 9-10, 70-80
West Virginia University, 78

Zamora, Lonnie, 20-29